FILE COPY

No: 580 a

Date 4th May 1995

Julia MacRae Books

Prickety Prackety

DIANA ROSS

with pictures by Caroline Crossland

Julia MacRae Books

LONDON SYDNEY AUCKLAND JOHANNESBURG

For William. C. C.

1 3 5 7 9 10 8 6 4 2

Text in this edition © 1995 Diana Ross
Illustrations © 1995 Caroline Crossland

Diana Ross and Caroline Crossland have asserted their rights
under the Copyright, Designs and Patents Act, 1988 to be
identified as the author and illustrator of this work

First published in the United Kingdom in 1995 by
Julia MacRae
Random House, 20 Vauxhall Bridge Road, London SW1V 2SA

Random House Australia (Pty) Limited
20 Alfred Street, Milsons Point, Sydney,
New South Wales 2061, Australia

Random House New Zealand Limited
18 Poland Road, Glenfield, Auckland 10, New Zealand

Random House South Africa (Pty) Limited
PO Box 337, Bergvlei 2012, South Africa

Random House UK Limited Reg. No. 954009

A CIP catalogue record for this book
is available from the British Library

ISBN 1–85681–600–1

Typeset by Deltatype Ltd, Ellesmere Port, Cheshire
Printed in China

THERE WAS once a hen called Prickety Prackety. She was a little golden brown bantam hen, and she walked about the garden on the tips of her toes – and she pecked here and pecked there and was busy the whole day long.

And once a day she felt like laying an egg.

Away she went to the hen-house, 'Cluck, Cluck, Cluck!' And she'd climb into the nesting box and fluff herself out and make gentle noises in her throat as soft as her own pretty feathers, and she'd sit, and she'd blink her eyes and go into a dozy-cosy and then, 'Cluck, Cluck, Cluck-a-Cluck-a-Cluck!'

What a surprise! What joy! An egg! A pretty brown speckeldy egg! Away she would go, not a thought in her head, peck here, peck there, on the tips of her toes.

And Anne would come at tea-time to collect the eggs, and when she saw the brown egg she would say,

'Oh! You good Mrs Prickety Prackety, you good little hen.'

Because Prickety Prackety was the only hen to lay brown eggs, so Anne knew that it was hers. And she would throw her out an extra handful of corn. One good turn deserves another.

But one day Prickety Prackety felt different. She felt like laying an egg. Oh, yes! But somehow not in the hen-house. So away she went by herself.

'Where are you going to, Prickety Prackety?' called Chanticleer the golden cock.

'I am going to mind my own business,' she said and tossed her head. Chanticleer ran and gave her a little peck, not a hard peck, but enough of a peck to show that although he loved her dearly he wouldn't let her answer him so rudely.

But Prickety Prackety paid no attention to him. She fluttered her feathers and cried 'Cloak!' because she knew he would expect it, and then she ran away, her head in the air.

'Prickety Prackety, where are you going?'

It was good sister Partlet, the old black hen, wanting her to share a dustbath near the cinder-pit.

'I am going to mind my own business,' said Prickety Prackety nodding pleasantly to Partlet, and Partlet ruffled the dust in her feathers and smiled to herself.

Prickety Prackety left the garden and came to the orchard. The grass was very green underneath the apple trees and the blossom was just coming out.

'Prickety Prackety, where are you going?' cried the white ducks rootling in the grass.

'I am going to mind my own business,' she said.

Beside the privet hedge was an old rusty drum.

It had been used last year to cover up the rhubarb, but now it was lying on its side and a jungle of nettles had grown up all round it.

And Prickety Prackety crept through the jungle of nettles, into the oil drum and clucked contentedly to find a few wisps of straw and dried grass. The geese and ducks smiled at each other and went on nibbling the grass in the orchard.

'Prickety Prackety has stolen a nest. I wonder if they will find it?' they thought to themselves.

Every day for twelve days Prickety Prackety disappeared into the oil drum.

Every day Chanticleer said, 'Prickety Prackety, where are you going?'

Every day Partlet said, 'Prickety Prackety, where are you going?'

Every day the geese and ducks said, 'Prickety Prackety, where are you going?'

And every day Prickety Prackety gave the same answer with a toss of the head. 'I am going to mind my own business.'

And every day at tea-time Anne would come in shaking her head.

'No eggs from Prickety Prackety. She's gone right off. And just when she was doing so well too.'

But worse was to come.

On the thirteenth day Prickety Prackety took a long drink and ate as much as she could when Anne put out the hot mash. And then she walked away looking *very* important.

'Where are you going, Prickety Prackety?' said Chanticleer.
'Where are you going, Prickety Prackety?' said Partlet.
'Where are you going, Prickety Prackety?' said the white ducks.

'Where are you going to, Prickety Prackety?' said the geese, following after her as if she were a procession.

But Prickety Prackety didn't even answer. She pranced along, her eyes shining.

That evening Anne came into the kitchen and said,
'Now I know why Prickety Prackety seemed to go off
laying. She has stolen a nest. I shall have to go and find it.'

So next day after she had put out the chicken food Anne began to look for Prickety Prackety.

She looked in the shrubbery. She looked in the vegetable garden. She looked in the sheds and outhouses. She looked along the hedges, looked in the orchard, but she didn't see Prickety Prackety, although Prickety Prackety saw her.

And every morning when it was first light and the other hens were still asleep shut up in the hen-house, Prickety Prackety would creep out of her jungle of nettles.

'Where are you going to, Prickety Prackety?' asked the little wild birds, the sparrows and finches, the blackbirds and the thrushes. But Prickety Prackety seemed not to hear, but would

peck here and peck there, gorging herself on grubs and grass and any remains of chicken food overlooked by the others. She would drink and drink from the bowl of water by the back door, and as she lifted her head the rising sun would shine into her eyes, and then back she would go through her jungle of nettles into the oil drum, and not the least glimpse of her to be seen when the rest of the world were about.

A week went by, and another, and the blossom on the apple trees was falling so that when the soft wind blew it looked like drifting snow. And still Prickety Prackety hid in her nest.

'Have you seen Prickety Prackety?' said Chanticleer to Partlet.

'Oh! She's around somewhere,' said Partlet, flaunting her feathers.

'Have you seen Prickety Prackety?'
said Partlet to the ducks.
    'Oh! I expect she's around
somewhere,' they said.

'Have you seen Prickety Prackety?'
asked the ducks of the geese.
    'We mind our own businessssssss,'
hissed the geese.

And Anne, in the kitchen yard, said, 'Now, let me see. It's gone all of two weeks since Prickety Prackety stole her nest. She ought to be out come Friday. I wonder how many will hatch?'

On Friday when the sun rose the sky was quiet and clear.

Prickety Prackety crept out into the orchard shaking the dew from the nettles as she passed, so she looked like a golden hen set with diamonds.

She pecked and pranced and pecked and drank, and cocked her eye at the sun, and then she went back to her eggs, her twelve brown eggs lying on the straw in the cool green shadow of the oil drum and nettles.

She stood, her head on one side, and listened.

Tap-tap, and the smooth round surface of the nearest egg was broken and a tiny jag of shell moved and was still.

'Cluck, Cluck, Cluck, Cluck!' crooned Prickety Prackety, deep in her throat and, very satisfied, she settled on her eggs.

That evening Anne went out at tea-time.

'Coop, Coop, Coop!' she cried, the corn measure in her hand, and from every side the hens came running.

'Coop, Coop, Coop!' cried Anne.

Then who should creep out of the nettles but Prickety Prackety. 'Cluck, Cluck, Cluck,' she said. And out of the nettles crept, one, two, three, four, five, six, seven, eight, nine, ten, eleven, twelve little tiny, tiny chicks, so small, so tiny,

so quick, so golden, so yellow – Oh, what a pretty sight!

'Well, you got them at last, Prickety Prackety,' said the geese.

'And very nice too,' said the ducks.

And Prickety Prackety led her family out of the orchard towards the yard. 'Coop, Coop, Coop, Coop,' cried Anne, scattering the corn.

But when she saw Prickety Prackety tripping towards her with one, two, three, four, five, six, seven, eight, nine, ten, eleven, twelve – yes, with twelve – tiny chicks, like little yellow clouds all about her,

'Oh!' she cried, and ran to the house.

'Caroline, Johnny, William, come quickly. Prickety Prackety has hatched her chicks.'

And everyone came running.

'Oh! Prickety Prackety, you *good* little hen!' And how they scattered the corn for her. But Anne was busy getting ready the special coop they kept for hens who had chicks; and they called it the Nursery Coop, for here the chicks would be safe from the cats and dogs and crows.

Very gently they lifted Prickety Prackety, and all the chicks
came running as she cried to them, 'Cluck, Cluck, Cluck!'
    'I reckon we don't run that fast when Mum calls us,' said
Anne – and the other children laughed. And they all helped to
carry the coop into the orchard, where the trees would

shade it. And when at last the children were gone Partlet came busily by.

'A lot of trouble, but worth it. They're a fine lot, Prickety Prackety.' And she nodded her head with approval.

And as for Chanticleer, he came stalking up glowing in the evening sun, and stood high on his toes, head cocked, looking at Prickety Prackety and the tiny heads poking in and out of her feathers. And then:

'Cock-a-Doooooodle Doooooooooo. Just look at my good wife, Prickety Prackety, and all our sons and daughters. Cock-a-Doooooodle Doooooooooo.'

It was like a fanfare of trumpets.

And Prickety Prackety blinked her eyes and smiled.